# MOODY PUMPKINS

By Janice K. Taylor

Illustrated by Leslie Weaver

Moody Pumpkins by Janice Taylor



Author Janice Taylor

ISBN #: 978-1-958792-09-4

# MOODY PUMPKINS

The pumpkins in the pumpkin patch
are ready for Halloween,
but for many different reasons,
they have a variety of moods.
Let's ask the pumpkins why
they are so moody.

Moody pumpkin, moody pumpkin,
what is your mood and why?


Today I am tearful.
A black cat made me cry.

Moody pumpkin, moody pumpkin,
what is your mood and why?


I feel spooked.
There is a haunted house nearby.

Moody pumpkin, moody pumpkin,
what is your mood and why?

Last night I felt glowing.
A full moon was in the sky.

Moody pumpkin, moody pumpkin,
what is your mood and why?

I am feeling frightened.
Three ghosts are flying by.

Moody pumpkin, moody pumpkin,
what is your mood and why?

Scared is how I feel.
I heard an owl screech from way up high.

Moody pumpkin, moody pumpkin,
what is your mood and why?

A spider sitting on top of me
is making me feel terrified.

Moody pumpkin, moody pumpkin,
what is your mood and why?

Right now I feel curious.
Where will I be in July?

Moody pumpkin, moody pumpkin,
what is your mood and why?

The frost makes me feel shivery,
a cold pumpkin did reply.

Moody pumpkin, moody pumpkin,
what is your mood and why?

Since I am the smallest pumpkin,
I feel bashful and shy.

Moody pumpkin, moody pumpkin,
what is your mood and why?

Lonely is how I feel,
one pumpkin said with a sigh.

Moody pumpkin, moody pumpkin,
what is your mood and why?

I am very cheerful,
so you won't see me cry.

Moody pumpkin, moody pumpkin,
what is your mood and why?

I'm in a goofy mood,
so I'm wearing a red neck tie.

Moody pumpkin, moody pumpkin,
what is your mood and why?

I feel so excited and
glad that you stopped by.

Moody pumpkin, moody pumpkin,
what is your mood and why?

Right now I feel so sleepy,
but I don't know why.

Moody pumpkin, moody pumpkin,
what is your mood and why?

I'm amazed after seeing such
a lovely butterfly.

Although the pumpkins have
many different moods, and
different reasons why,
they all feel very thrilled
that Halloween is nearby!

# The End.

# About the Author

Author Janice K. Taylor lives in Columbus, Indiana, with her husband and their toy poodle, Bailey.

She is a graduate of Indiana University, where she obtained her degrees in Elementary Education and Library Science. She taught for many years in Columbus and was also an elementary librarian for several years. She is currently retired and enjoys traveling, boating, clogging, knitting, walks with Bailey and, of course, reading and writing.

# About the Illustrator

Illustrator Leslie Weaver is a native of Columbus, Indiana, where she resides with her husband Ben.

Leslie has a Bachelor's Degree in Art Education from Purdue University and a Master's in Education from Indiana Wesleyan. She currently teaches art classes at Columbus North High School and has her own art business, LEW's Landing. Her artwork can be viewed at lewslanding.com.

Leslie and her husband stay very active competing in triathlons and running events. They combine their active lives and their love of travel by competing in race events around the United States. Her summers are spent gardening, training, and relaxing by the pool.

Now the pumpkins have shared
their moods and feelings,
what is your mood today and why?